ONCE UPON A FAIRY TALE

The Missing Dwarf

STORY BY
**Anna
Staniszewski**

ART BY
**Macky
Pamintuan**

BRANCHES™

SCHOLASTIC INC.

Help Kara and Zed fix all the fairy tales!

TABLE OF CONTENTS

For Lia — AS
For Ali, my brave princess — MP

Text copyright © 2020 by Anna Staniszewski
Illustrations copyright © 2020 by Scholastic Inc.

Cover photos © Shutterstock: font (Idea Trader), stiches (KariDesign), texture (1028.art), (ailin1), (Hitdelight), (Tokarchuk Andrii), (vi mart).

Library of Congress Cataloging-in-Publication Data

Names: Staniszewski, Anna, author. | Pamintuan, Macky, illustrator.
Title: The missing dwarf / by Anna Staniszewski ; illustrated by Macky Pamintuan.
Description: First edition. | New York, NY : Branches/Scholastic Inc., 2020. |
Series: Once upon a fairy tale ; 3 | Summary: Snow White's wedding is only a day away, but Ralph, one of the seven dwarfs, has disappeared and it looks like the evil queen may have kidnapped him; Kara and Zed volunteer to rescue him, with Zed's pet sheep Lilly tagging along, but things are not quite what they seem—and it is up to the timid Lilly to save them all from the fashion-challenged queen.
Identifiers: LCCN 2019010239| ISBN 9781338349795 (hardcover) |
ISBN 9781338349788 (pbk.)
Subjects: LCSH: Snow White (Tale)—Juvenile fiction. | Dwarfs (Folklore)—Juvenile fiction. | Missing persons—Juvenile fiction. | Sheep—Juvenile fiction. | Queens—Juvenile fiction. | Fashion—Juvenile fiction. | Fantasy. | CYAC: Characters in literature—Fiction. | Dwarfs (Folklore)—Fiction. | Missing persons—Fiction. | Kings, queens, rulers, etc.—Fiction. | Fashion—Fiction. | LCGFT: Fantasy fiction. | Humorous fiction.
Classification: LCC PZ7.S78685 Mi 2020 | DDC 813.6 [Fic] —dc23
LC record available at https://lccn.loc.gov/2019010239

10 9 8 7 6 5 4 3 2 1

20 21 22 23 24

Printed in China   62
First edition, April 2020
Book design by Sarah Dvojack

1

The Seven Dwarfs

"**K**ara! Someone is here to see you," her father said. He poked his head through the doorway to the storeroom. "Where are you?"

"Back here!" Kara called loudly from behind a stack of boots.

Suddenly, there was a crash from the front of the store.

Kara ran out of the storeroom after her father. They rushed to the front of her parents' shoe shop, where they found a display tipped over. There was a woolly sheep underneath.

Two fairy customers were hurrying out of the shop, and Kara's mother did *not* look happy. Nearby, Kara's best friend Zed stood, looking embarrassed.

"What happened?" Kara asked him.

"Loud noises make Lilly a little jumpy," Zed explained. He turned to the sheep and added softly, "You can come out now, Lilly."

Slowly, the sheep crawled out from under the pile of shoes. There was a clog hanging from her nose.

"Where did Lilly come from?" Kara asked as she helped Zed clean up the mess.

"She was outside our barn this morning," Zed explained. "Gram says if I don't find a home for Lilly soon, I'll have to split my meals with her!"

Kara chuckled. Zed loved taking in stray animals. But if there was one thing Zed liked more than that, it was eating.

When the shoe display was up again, Kara's parents nodded in approval. Then they went back to helping their startled customers.

Zed took a scroll out of his bag. As a royal messenger, he delivered letters all over the Enchanted Kingdom.

"Do you want to come with me to drop off a message for the Seven Dwarfs?" he asked Kara.

"Of course I do!" Kara said. She had read about the famous Seven Dwarfs in the *Enchanted Times*. With their help, Snow White had escaped her stepmother, the Evil Queen, and met her prince. Now Snow White's wedding was only a day away!

"Is it all right if I go with Zed?" Kara asked her parents.

"Yes," Kara's mother said as she zipped up a troll's boots. "Just be home before dark."

Kara waved to her parents and followed Zed and Lilly out the door.

"I'm glad I won't have to deliver this message alone," Zed said. "The Seven Dwarfs live in the Deep Dark Woods."

"So?" Kara asked.

"It's *dark* in there!" Zed cried. "Who knows what kind of monsters live in that forest?"

At the word *monster*, Lilly bleated nervously.

Kara laughed and rubbed Lilly's head. "Don't worry," she told Zed. "I'll protect both of you."

Into the
Deep Dark Woods

The Deep Dark Woods were smaller than they sounded, but they *were* dark. Even though it was still morning, the sun was hidden behind thick trees. Zed and Lilly stayed glued to Kara's side, jumping at every sound.

Finally, the trees thinned. The path brought Kara and Zed to a small cottage.

Zed went to the door, ready to deliver his message. They heard panicked shouting coming from inside. Lilly hid behind Zed, her eyes wide.

"It sounds like something is wrong," Kara said.

Zed knocked, and the door flew open. A well-dressed dwarf looked back at them. "Oh," he said, his face falling. "You're not Ralph."

"Who's Ralph?" Kara asked.

"Our brother," another dwarf said, coming up beside him. "He's missing."

A third dwarf popped his head through the door. Kara noticed that he was wearing the same stylish red hat as the other two. He said, "We all woke up this morning, ready to go off to work, and hi ho, hi ho—uh-oh!"

"Ralph wasn't in his bed!" the second dwarf said. "He disappeared during the night!"

"When did you last see him?" Kara asked.

But the first dwarf frowned at her. "Wait, who are you two?" he asked. He seemed the tallest—and the grumpiest—of the bunch.

"I'm Zed, a royal messenger," Zed said. "And this is Kara. We have a letter for you."

The dwarf snatched the message out of Zed's hand. "It must be from Ralph!" he said. He opened it, and his shoulders drooped. "It's just about our suits for the wedding."

Suddenly a voice came from behind Kara and Zed: "So Ralph really *is* gone?"

They turned to see a young woman standing on the path. She was wearing a stylish dress and a fabulous hat. Her shoes were so fancy that Kara knew even her parents would be impressed.

"Snow, what are you doing here?" the first dwarf asked.

"I came as soon as I learned Ralph was missing," she said as she walked toward the cottage.

"But how did you know?" another dwarf asked. "We just found out ourselves."

Snow White held up a piece of paper. "This note was on my doorstep this morning," she said.

Kara squinted. "What's that goo all over it?" she asked.

"It's hat glue," Snow White said. "I spilled it by accident. But I can still read most of what the note says."

"What *does* it say?" one of the other dwarfs asked. "What happened to our brother?"

"I'm afraid Ralph has been kidnapped!" Snow White cried.

Kidnapped!

"**R**alph's been kidnapped?" the first dwarf repeated. "By who?"

"It was the Evil Queen," Snow White said.

She held out the piece of paper, and the tallest dwarf took it. He struggled to read the glue-covered note.

All the dwarfs gasped.

"This must be the queen's plan to ruin my wedding," Snow White said. "She kidnapped Ralph. And I think she took my favorite pony, too! I had to walk all the way here."

"We'll go after her and get Ralph back!" one of the dwarfs cried.

"It is too dangerous," Snow White said. "What if the queen kidnaps *all* of you?"

"Send your guards after her!" a dwarf said.

Snow White shook her head. "I can't," she said. "They're busy preparing for tomorrow's wedding. And there's no one else who can help. I . . . I don't know what to do!"

"Zed and I will go see the queen!" Kara cried.

"Kara!" Zed said in a loud whisper. "Did you hear the part about it being *dangerous*?"

"We'll bring Ralph back in time for the wedding." How could Kara resist? It sounded like an adventure *and* a chance to see the Evil Queen's castle.

Snow White hesitated. "You two are awfully young to be rescuing anyone," she said.

"Just because someone is small doesn't mean they can't help," the shortest dwarf chimed in. The top of his head barely reached Kara's shoulder.

"That's true," Snow White said slowly.

"We already helped Princess Aspen fix her broken mirror and Prince Patrick find his missing slipper," Kara said. "We can help you, too!"

"So *you're* the pair I've been hearing so much about," Snow White said. She sounded impressed. "If you really wish to help, I won't stop you. But please, be careful."

"We always are!" Kara said as Zed rolled his eyes. "Don't worry. We'll find Ralph in no time!"

4

Another Red Hat

Kara and Zed headed farther into the Deep Dark Woods. Lilly trotted close behind them.

"How will we find the Evil Queen's castle?" Zed asked, dragging his feet.

"Easy," Kara said. She pulled a map out of her pocket. "See? It's just on the other side of the woods. If we hurry there and find Ralph right away, we can still be home before dark."

A little while later, the path turned. As they went around a tree, Zed tripped on a half-eaten apple and—

"Ah!" Zed cried as he landed in the dirt.

"That's strange," Kara said. "I didn't think green apples grew around here."

"Forget the apple!" Zed said as he scrambled to his feet. "Lilly is making a run for it!"

Zed's cry had spooked Lilly, and now the sheep was bolting away.

Kara and Zed ran after her. Soon they came to a bridge with a brook running under it. Lilly was clearly too scared by the sound of the water to cross.

Together, Kara and Zed coaxed her toward the path.

When they were back on the trail, Kara noticed a tall red hat in the dirt. "Zed, look!" Kara said. "The other dwarfs were wearing hats just like this. It must belong to Ralph!"

Zed frowned. "Does that mean the queen brought him this way?" he asked.

"Yes!" Kara said. "Maybe he dropped it on purpose, so we could track him."

"But . . . what will we *do* once we find him?" Zed asked. "We're no match for the Evil Queen. She's magical!"

"That's true," Kara admitted. "But we will figure something out."

Zed groaned. "Or the Evil Queen will turn us into toads," he said. "I really don't want to eat bugs!"

Just then, Kara heard rustling nearby. She scanned the woods and spotted a man between the trees. He was holding a bow and arrow, and he was looking right at her!

5

The Evil Queen's Castle

"**Z**ed," Kara whispered, nodding toward the trees. "Someone's over there."

"Where?" Zed said. He looked where Kara had pointed.

When Kara turned back, the man was gone.

Kara and Zed kept moving along the path with their eyes wide open. There was no sign of the man with the bow and arrow. And there was no sign of the queen or Ralph, either.

Finally they spotted the Evil Queen's castle in the distance. It was so tall and thin that it almost disappeared into the clouds.

"We'll sneak inside and look for Ralph. The queen probably put him in the dungeons," Kara said.

Zed gulped. "Dungeons?" he asked. "We don't have to go down there, do we?"

Kara simply pulled Zed along, with Lilly trotting after them.

Near the castle, they hid behind some bushes to get a better look. A drawbridge led up to the castle. Two giant bears in armor stood guard on either side. Below the bridge was a wide moat.

"Do you think there are crocodiles in the moat?" Zed asked nervously.

"No way," Kara said.

Zed sighed in relief.

"Crocodiles don't live in this area," Kara added. "But there might be alligators."

"Alligators?" Zed squealed.

"We shouldn't try to swim. We will have to distract the guards and cross the bridge," Kara said.

Just then, a bird squawked above their heads. Lilly jumped at the sound and took off—toward the moat!

"She's heading for the bridge!" Zed cried.

The guards yelled at Lilly to stop, but she kept running. Kara and Zed tried to catch up to Lilly, but it was too late.

Before they knew it, all three of them were on the bears' shoulders, being carried across the drawbridge.

"Any chance you are bringing us to the dungeons?" Kara asked hopefully.

"Quiet," one of the guards growled as they entered the Evil Queen's castle.

6

Too Quiet

The inside of the Evil Queen's castle was quiet. Very quiet. *Too* quiet.

Guards and servants tiptoed through the corridors. It seemed as if the entire castle were holding its breath.

Kara held her breath, too, as the guards hurried her and Zed along.

"Where are we going?" Zed asked.

"Shh!" the guards answered.

They passed a huge library. Kara wished she had time to look at all the books inside! Finally they stopped at a wooden door. When it opened, Kara saw another bear sitting at a large desk.

Unlike the guards, he was in a crisp suit and a surprisingly tall hat.

"We found these three storming the castle," one of the guards said in a soft voice.

"Thank you," the bear said and waved the guards away. He turned to Kara and Zed and bared his teeth. "Hello, I am Marty," he whispered. "I'm the queen's assistant."

"I'm Kara. This is Zed and his sheep, Lilly," Kara said. She tried not to look at Marty's sharp fangs.

"A-are you going to eat us?" Zed asked the bear. Lilly cowered behind him.

Marty laughed softly. "No. I just had a snack. But please, keep your voices down. The queen likes her home quiet these days. It calms her."

No wonder it sounds like everyone is asleep, Kara thought.

Marty looked them over curiously. "People usually try to break *out* of the castle, not *into* it. Why are you here?" he asked.

Kara cleared her throat. "We're looking for one of the Seven Dwarfs," she said.

"*Baaa!*" Lilly added.

"The dwarf's name is Ralph," Zed said. "He was kidnapped by the queen."

Marty blinked in surprise. "What makes you think the *queen* kidnapped him?" he asked.

"She left a note on Snow White's doorstep," Kara said. "She wrote that she was bringing Ralph here."

Marty shook his head. "The queen hasn't left the castle since she heard Snow White was getting married," he said. "She couldn't have kidnapped anyone."

"We found Ralph's hat on the road to the castle," Zed said. "We *know* he's here."

"That's impossible!" Marty roared. Then he covered his mouth with his paw.

The yelling was too much for Lilly. She let out a terrified bleat. Then she turned and bolted out the door.

7

Yum, Apples!

"Lilly, come back!" Zed said. But she had already disappeared down the hall.

"We have to find that sheep before the queen does!" Marty said in an urgent whisper.

Kara nodded and followed Zed out the door. Marty tiptoed after them. They hurried down a long hallway lined with purple-curtained doorways.

"Baaa!" Lilly's bleat echoed from down the hall.

"She's in here somewhere," Zed said.

"What is this place?" Kara asked. She read a label on the doorway closest to her: SHOES.

"This hallway holds all the queen's closets," Marty explained. "She keeps her most treasured things here."

Down the hall, Lilly let out another echoing *"Baaa!"*

"Hurry, we need to find that sheep," Marty said. He pulled back the curtain on a doorway labeled STATUES.

"Wow," Kara said as dozens of stone eyes stared back at her.

"They're all of the queen," Marty explained.

She really is beautiful, Kara thought.

"Lilly is not here," Zed said. "Let's try the next one."

The SPELLS closet was lined with shelves. On one, Kara spotted a silver comb and a sack of shiny red apples. These had to be the items the queen had used to try to poison Snow White.

"Yum, apples," Zed said. He reached out to take one.

"Zed!" Kara cried. She pulled his hand away. "Do you want to get poisoned?"

"No, I guess not," Zed grumbled.

They continued down the hall, ducking into closets. One was full of jewels. Another was packed with hats. Yet another was bursting with gowns.

"Careful!" Marty said, pulling Kara away from the last curtain. "The queen doesn't allow *anyone* to touch her dresses." He suddenly sounded afraid.

"What will happen if she finds us here?" Kara asked.

Marty let out a sad sigh and took off his hat. Underneath were one regular bear ear and one extra-long bear ear.

"Ever since Snow White left, the queen's magic has been on the fritz," Marty explained. "Now when she gets upset, magic shoots out all over the place, and *this* sort of thing happens."

Zed's eyes widened. "We better find Lilly and get out of ear," he said to Kara. "I mean *here*!"

Just then, they heard a deep voice say, "*You* are the fairest of them all!"

The voice echoed from the end of the hall. Kara and Zed hurried toward the sound. They ducked into the last closet. Inside was a giant gold mirror.

Lilly stood in front of it, admiring her reflection.

"There you are!" Zed cried.

Suddenly a hiss came from the other end of the hallway: "Who is using my magic mirror?"

Kara and Zed looked at each other. The Evil Queen was coming!

The Queen's Mirror

The curtain to the Mirror Room flung open, and the queen walked in. She was as tall and thin as her castle. She was also wearing the strangest outfit Kara had ever seen. *It looks like she got dressed in the dark*, Kara thought.

"Where is she?" the queen asked. Her voice was so quiet, it almost sounded loud. "Where is my stepdaughter?" Kara noticed that she kept her eyes turned away from the magic mirror.

"Your Majesty," Marty said with a bow. "Snow White isn't here."

The queen looked Kara and Zed up and down. "I doubt either of *you* could be the fairest in the land," she said.

"Hey!" Zed said. "My gram says I'm handsome."

"We weren't using your magic mirror, Your Majesty," Kara jumped in. "It was our sheep."

"*Baaa,*" Lilly added.

The queen sniffed and turned to Marty. "Who are these children? Why is there a sheep in my Mirror Room?" she asked. "And why are they all being so *noisy*?"

"Kara and Zed are looking for a dwarf named Ralph," Marty explained.

"Well, they won't find him here," the queen said. She turned to leave.

"Wait!" Kara cried.

The queen hissed. Kara quickly lowered her voice to an urgent whisper. "Your Majesty," she went on. "If *you* didn't kidnap Ralph, then who sent Snow White that mean note?"

"It wasn't me," the queen said. "If I were to kidnap anyone, it would be *Snow White*. I've been a mess without her. I can't even look at myself in the mirror anymore!"

"Why not?" Zed asked.

"Isn't it obvious?" the queen answered, her voice rising. She pointed to her mismatched clothes. "Look at me!"

Everyone gasped as the queen's fingers all started to glow with magic.

"Watch out!" Marty cried.

"Baaa!" Lilly squeaked.

A beam of bright light burst out of the queen's fingers. It bounced off the mirror and shot straight at Marty's head. Instantly his smaller ear started to grow. Soon he looked more like a giant rabbit than a bear.

At the sight of her mixed-up magic, the queen's anger seemed to vanish. "I'm going back to bed," she whispered in a tired voice. Then she shuffled out of the room and down the hall.

Marty looked at himself in the mirror. "At least my ears match now," he said sadly before pulling his hat back on.

"Wait, where's Lilly?" Zed asked. There was no sign of the sheep.

"She must have run off again," Kara said with a sigh.

Before Kara and Zed could start searching for Lilly, a guard hurried into the Mirror Room. Instead of a bear tail, she had a bright peacock tail. "Someone has broken into Snow White's old bedroom!" the guard whispered.

Snow White's Bedroom

"**C**ome with me," Marty told Kara and Zed.

"Where are we going?" Kara asked.

"I need to check Snow White's room. If someone broke in, things could have been stolen," Marty said. "But I'm not letting you two out of my sight."

"We have to find our sheep," Zed protested.

"And we still need to find Ralph, too," Kara added.

"Later," Marty growled. "Now come along. And *be quiet*."

Kara and Zed had no choice but to follow him and the guard.

"Don't worry," Kara whispered to Zed. "I'm sure Lilly is fine."

They wove through the halls of the silent castle.

"I'm confused," Kara couldn't help saying. "Why does the queen want Snow White to come back to the castle? I thought they hated each other."

Marty sighed. "The queen was jealous of her stepdaughter's beauty," he said. "She was angry when the magic mirror said Snow White was the fairest in the land. But the queen also relied on her."

"How?" Zed asked.

"Snow White used to be the queen's personal fashion designer," Marty explained. "The queen is lost without Snow's style advice. It's affecting her confidence—and her magic."

Kara remembered the queen's strange outfit. No wonder she didn't want to look at herself in the mirror.

They turned a corner and finally reached Snow White's bedroom. When they went inside, Kara felt like she was in a museum. Sketches of beautiful gowns, hats, and shoes lined the walls. *Snow White sure is talented*, Kara thought.

But the room was also a mess. All the drawers were open, and a couple of chairs had been knocked over. Two more guards were looking around for clues.

"Is anything missing?" Marty asked a guard.

One of the guard's legs looked like a mop. Clearly, no one was safe from the queen's magic.

"No, sir," the guard replied. "But the window was broken."

"We think we know who is responsible," a second guard chimed in. "Someone saw a dwarf climbing the tower."

Kara and Zed looked at each other. "A *dwarf*?" they said at once.

Searching for Something

"**I** knew it!" Kara said excitedly. "Ralph is at the castle! The Evil Queen *did* kidnap him!"

"But if the queen kidnapped him, he would be a prisoner. He wouldn't be breaking *into* the castle," Zed said.

Kara paused. "Maybe you're right," she said.

She took out the hat she had found in the woods. It matched one of the designs on Snow White's wall. Kara had thought Ralph left the hat behind so they could follow him. Now she wasn't so sure.

"Search the castle for that dwarf," Marty told the guards. "We need to find him before he breaks in anywhere else." Then he turned to Kara and Zed. "As for you two," he said, "please get your sheep and leave. You've caused enough trouble."

The guards hurried away, and Marty followed after them.

When they were gone, Kara paced the room. "If the queen didn't kidnap Ralph, then why is he here?" she asked.

"Snow White's bedroom is such a mess! Maybe he was searching for something," Zed said, glancing at the open dresser drawers.

"But what?" Kara asked. Then she spotted an apple core by the window. It was from a green apple, like the one they saw in the woods. She went over and nudged it with her toe. "Do you think Ralph could have left this here?"

Zed shrugged. "Maybe. At least I didn't trip over it this time," he said. Then he sighed. "We should go find Lilly before the queen zaps us with her wonky magic, too."

At that moment, Kara noticed something out the window. "Zed, look," she said, pointing at the ground below.

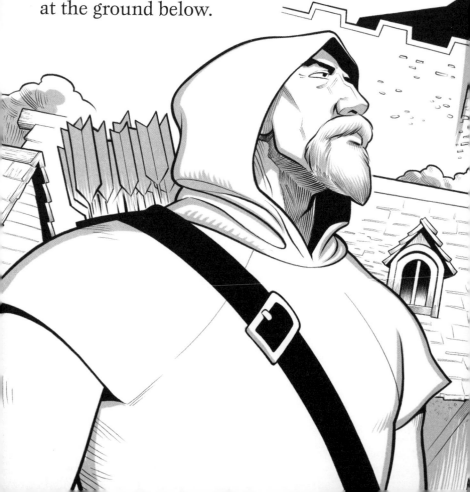

A man with a bow and arrow stood next to the stables. He seemed to be looking up at her.

"That's the same man I saw in the woods," Kara went on. "I think he's following us!"

"But why?" Zed asked.

Kara smiled. "Let's go find out," she said. Then she pulled Zed into the hall and toward the stables.

11

To the Stables

When Kara and Zed reached the stables, the man with the bow and arrow was gone—again.

They checked each stall, but they only found a few bored-looking horses.

"Where did he go?" Zed asked, flopping onto a bale of hay.

Kara slumped down next to him.

"Hey, look!" Zed said. He pointed behind the hay to an empty sack and some green apple cores. Next to them was a stylish coat. It looked like the ones Ralph's brothers had been wearing that morning.

"Ralph *is* here!" Kara said. "He must have brought a sack of apples with him to eat along the way."

"Wait a minute," Zed said. He got to his feet and walked over to the next stall. "This pony has the wrong royal seal."

Kara went to take a look. "Snow White said her pony was missing! Remember?" she said to Zed. "She thought the queen took it. But *Ralph* must have taken the pony and ridden it here!"

"If Ralph came to the castle on his own, he might not even know people are looking for him," Zed added.

Kara paced in front of the stall, trying to think. The pony's eyes followed her as she went back and forth. "If Ralph's not a prisoner, then the queen really didn't write that note to Snow White," Kara realized. She stopped pacing and sucked in a breath. "*Ralph* must have left it!"

Zed wrinkled his forehead. "Why would Ralph write to Snow White and tell her he was kidnapping himself?" he asked.

"He didn't," Kara said. "We couldn't read the whole note, remember? Snow White had spilled glue on it."

"So what did it really say?" Zed wondered.

"Ralph was probably just telling Snow White that he was heading to the queen's castle," Kara decided. "His note said something about a wedding present . . . I bet he came here to find one for her!"

"*That's* what he was looking for in Snow White's room!" Zed said. He clapped in excitement. Then he lowered his hands. "Wait. But  the guards said that nothing was missing."

"True," Kara said, tapping her chin with her finger. "If Ralph left the pony here, that means he's still at the castle. Whatever he's looking for, he hasn't found it yet."

Suddenly Kara saw a flash of movement out the stable window. She stood on her tiptoes to look outside.

The man with the bow and arrow was crouched nearby, listening to their conversation. This time, she was not going to let him get away!

The Mysterious Man

Kara and Zed snuck up behind the mysterious man.

"Why are you following us?" Kara demanded.

The man jumped up in surprise. "You two were not supposed to see me," he said. He sounded embarrassed. "I'd promised to follow you in secret."

"Who told you to follow us?" Zed asked.

"Snow White," the man said. "She was worried about you facing the Evil Queen. She asked me to keep an eye on you."

"Wait," Kara said. "I remember reading about a huntsman before . . . Are you the huntsman who helped Snow White escape the queen?"

The man nodded. "I worked for the queen for a long time, but I've known Snow White since she was a baby. I promised to help Snow in her new life with the prince." He glanced at the castle. "Have you found Ralph?"

"No, but we know he is here somewhere,"
Zed said. "He's been leaving apple cores all over
the place."

"We think he came to the castle to find a wedding present for Snow White," Kara added. "He broke into Snow White's old bedroom, but whatever he was looking for wasn't there."

"Did he break into Snow's studio, too?" the huntsman asked.

"Her studio?" Zed repeated.

"It's near the library," the huntsman said. "Snow did most of her designing and sewing for the queen there."

Kara gasped. "That must be where Ralph is going next!" she said.

13
Snow White's Studio

To get back into the castle, Kara used Ralph's coat and hat to disguise the huntsman.

"We're still looking for our sheep," Zed told the guards at the drawbridge. "Our friend is helping us find her."

The bears growled as they looked over the huntsman. His disguise didn't quite cover his bow and arrows. But luckily, the bears didn't seem to notice. They waved them all across the bridge.

Once inside the castle, the huntsman removed his disguise. Then they all headed toward the library. Kara, Zed, and the huntsman started quietly opening doors. There was no sign of Lilly or Ralph. But soon they discovered a room filled with sewing supplies and fabrics.

"We found Snow White's studio!" Zed said.

It is even more colorful than my parents' shoe shop, Kara thought.

They went inside, keeping an eye out for Ralph. But no one was there.

"Wait!" Kara said, spotting an apple core on the floor. "Another green apple!"

"Ralph *was* here!" Zed said.

"If he found what he was looking for, he's probably headed home by now," the huntsman said.

Zed groaned. "Tracking down a dwarf is hard work!" he said, leaning against a dress form. As soon as Zed touched it, it crashed to the floor and broke in half.

"Zed!" Kara cried.

"I'm sorry!" Zed whispered. "I'll be more careful."

"No, look!" Kara said. Tucked inside the dress form was a small notebook.

"That's Snow's sketchbook!" the huntsman said. "She never went anywhere without it. But she had to leave it behind when she escaped the castle."

"This must be what Ralph is looking for!" Kara said.

Just then, they heard the magic mirror's deep voice echoing down the hall: "You are *not* the fairest dwarf of them all!"

Kara smiled. "Ralph must be in the Mirror Room!"

"Let's go!" Zed said.

14
Don't Eat That!

Kara and Zed rushed back toward the queen's closets. The huntsman followed them. They turned down the purple hallway and ran to the Mirror Room.

They found Ralph standing right in front of the mirror. In his hand was a piece of shiny red fruit.

It was one of the queen's poisoned apples!

"No!" Kara cried. "Don't eat—"

Just then, the huntsman lifted his bow and aimed it at Ralph! The arrow whooshed through the air. But instead of hitting Ralph, it went right through the poisoned apple. The apple flew out of Ralph's hand and ended up pinned to the wall beside him.

"Hey!" Ralph said. "I was going to eat that."

"Trust me," Zed told him. "You wouldn't have liked it."

Ralph looked at Kara and Zed. "I know the huntsman, but who are you two?" Ralph asked.

"I'm Kara, and this is Zed," Kara explained. "Snow White thought you'd been kidnapped. We came to rescue you."

"Kidnapped?" Ralph repeated in surprise. "But my note explained everything."

"Snow White spilled glue on your note," Zed said. "She couldn't read the whole thing."

"She thought the queen was trying to ruin her wedding," Kara added.

"Oh no," Ralph said. "I only came here to get—"

"Snow's sketchbook?" Kara interrupted. She handed him the book.

Ralph's face lit up. "Yes!" he cried. "She'll be so happy to see it again! Where did you find it?"

Before Kara could answer, the queen burst in with Marty at her side.

"Who is making all this *noise*?" the queen hissed. Then she spotted the huntsman. "You! I fired you after you helped Snow White escape!" She looked at Ralph. "And you! You're one of Snow White's dwarfs!"

"Snow didn't want to be your stylist anymore," the huntsman said.

"And I'm here to take back what belongs to her," Ralph said. He hugged the sketchbook to his chest.

The Evil Queen's eyes widened. "Snow's sketchbook!" she said. She was no longer whispering. She was shouting.

"Your Majesty," Marty pleaded, "try to stay calm."

But the queen ignored him. "Give me that sketchbook!" she demanded. "If I have Snow's designs, I can be fashionable again—all on my own!"

"I'm not giving you anything!" Ralph said.

"That sketchbook belongs to Snow White," the huntsman said, raising his bow.

"No, it is MINE!" the queen roared. Her fingers started to glow, brighter and brighter, until they looked like they were on fire.

"Watch out!" Kara said.

"Everybody, cover your ears!" Zed cried.

But before anyone could move, a creature burst through the doorway!

The Fairest of Them All

Lilly stood in the doorway to the Mirror Room. She was covered from head to hoof in the queen's dresses and scarves and jewels.

The queen's eyes widened at the sight. Kara was afraid she'd zap Lilly with her magic. But all of a sudden, the queen's fingers stopped glowing. "That outfit looks amazing!" she said to the sheep. "You have quite the eye for fashion!"

"Baaa!" Lilly said, looking at herself in the magic mirror.

"Come with me!" the queen said, waving for the sheep to follow her. The two of them rushed out of the Mirror Room.

Zed, Kara, and their new friends exchanged confused looks. Soon they heard bleats and laughter coming from down the hall. What were Lilly and the queen doing? Was Lilly all right?

A minute later, the queen ran into the Mirror Room again. She was wearing the outfit Lilly had picked out. And she was smiling!

Lilly came in after her in a tutu and a rain hat.

"I feel fabulous!" the queen said. She strode over to her magic mirror. "Mirror, mirror on the wall. Who is the fairest of them all?"

"Snow White is the fairest of them all," the mirror said.

The queen sighed. "Yes, I know. But who is the fairest *after* Snow White?" she asked.

"You are, my queen," the mirror replied.

"I'm myself again!" the queen cried. She lifted her hand and aimed it at Marty. It began to glow . . .

"Your Majesty, no!" Marty cried. He covered his head.

A beam of light shot out of the queen's fingers. Then Marty's ears started to shrink. They grew smaller and smaller until they were just the right size.

"That's better," the queen said. She turned to Lilly. "You *must* be my new stylist."

There was a moment of stunned silence.

"But your majesty," Zed said. "Lilly can't be your new stylist. She hates loud noises and—"

"We always keep things quiet here at the castle," the queen said. "And I'll do anything for fashion." She petted Lilly's head, and the sheep cuddled up to her.

"We'll take good care of your sheep," Marty said. "I promise."

"Just think," Kara told Zed. "Now that Lilly found a new home, your gram won't make you share your meals with her."

Zed's face brightened. "That's true!" he said.

Then the queen rushed off with Lilly happily trotting after her.

"Good-bye, Lilly," Zed said with a wave.

Marty cleared his throat. "Since you have found Ralph, maybe it's time for you to head home?" he asked.

Kara smiled. "You're right," she said. "We have a wedding to get to!"

Apple-y Ever After

The next day, Snow White's wedding went off without a hitch. All the Seven Dwarfs were there, lined up in their matching suits. And Snow White wore the most stylish gown Kara had ever seen.

"Look at all these amazing shoes!" Kara said to Zed as they walked through the party after the wedding.

"I'm glad Snow White let us borrow some fancy clothes," Zed said, adjusting his collar.

Just then, Snow White came over with Ralph at her side. She was holding her favorite sketchbook, and there were tears in her eyes. "Thank you, Kara and Zed," she said. "Without you, this wedding never would have happened."

"And I couldn't have found Snow's perfect gift without your help," Ralph added.

"We were lucky our sheep and the queen had so much in common," Zed said.

"Plus, it was fun," Kara added.

Snow White gave them a grateful nod. Then she pulled Ralph away to dance with the prince and the other dwarfs.

"I don't know how you could call yesterday *fun*," Zed said to Kara. "We almost got eaten by bears and zapped with magic and—"

"And we solved the mystery and had an adventure," Kara finished. "It was great!"

"But we barely ate anything!" Zed grumbled.

"Do you want an apple?" Kara asked, pulling a green one out from behind her back.

Zed groaned and held his stomach. "I never want to see another apple again!" he said. Then his eyes lit up as he scanned the dessert table. "Ooh! Is that apple pie?"

Kara laughed. "Let's go have a slice and celebrate," she said. So they did.

About the Creators

Anna Staniszewski is the author of over a dozen books for young readers, including *Secondhand Wishes* and *Dogosauraus Rex*. She lives outside Boston with her family and teaches at Simmons University. She shares both Kara's love of reading and Zed's love of dessert.

Macky Pamintuan was born in the Philippines. He received his bachelor of fine arts in San Francisco, and he has illustrated numerous children's books. He has a smarty-pants young daughter who loves to read and go on imaginary adventures with her furry pal and trusty sidekick, Winter. He now lives in Mexico with his family.

Once Upon a Fairy Tale

The Missing Dwarf

Questions and Activities

Kara and Zed look everywhere for Ralph! Name at least two clues they find that lead them to the missing dwarf.

Ralph came to the castle looking for Snow White's sketchbook. Which two rooms did he search? Where did Kara finally find it? Reread chapters 9 and 12.

When the queen's magic backfires, it can transform the people and animals around her. Find three examples of her mixed-up magic in the story.

In chapter 14, Ralph almost eats a poison apple. How does the huntsman stop him?

Pretend you are a fashion designer like Snow White. Make your own sketchbook. Then draw new clothes and outfits you could wear!

scholastic.com/branches